Chapter One

"Wake up, Cinderelly!" a little voice squeaked. "It's late!"

Cinderella sat straight up in bed. "Oh, my goodness!" she said to her mouse friend Gus. "Did I oversleep? I need to make breakfast, and feed the chickens, and start the . . ."

Her voice trailed off as she looked around her. Instead of being in a drafty old attic, she was in a large, bright, and sunny room. She no longer slept under a thin blanket. She was nestled under a soft down quilt, a pile of fluffy pillows behind her head. Cinderella sighed with relief.

"Gus-Gus," scolded a mouse named Suzy. "Cinderelly doesn't need to wake up early! She's a princess now."

Gus looked down bashfully and twisted his nightcap in his paws. "Sorry, sorry," he said. "I forgot!"

Cinderella smiled at the plump little mouse. "That's all right, Gus," she said. "We haven't been living in the castle all that long. I sometimes forget that we don't live with my stepfamily anymore, too."

Jaq made a tiny fist and shook it in the air. "Terrible Tremaines!" he exclaimed.

Cinderella
The Lost Tiara

By Kitty Richards
Illustrated by Studio IBOIX

DISNEP PRESS
New York

Copyright © 2012 Disney Enterprises, Inc. All rights reserved.
Published by Disney Press, an imprint of Disney Book Group.
No part of this book may be reproduced or transmitted in any form
or by any means, electronic or mechanical, including photocopying,
recording, or by any information storage and retrieval system,
without written permission from the publisher.
For information address Disney Press,
114 Fifth Avenue, New York, New York 10011-5690.

Printed in the United States of America
First Edition
1 3 5 7 9 10 8 6 4 2
G658-7729-4-12167
Library of Congress Catalog Card Number: 2012936584

ISBN 978-1-4231-5197-5

For more Disney Press fun, visit www.disneybooks.com

If you purchased this book without a cover, you should be aware that
this book is stolen property. It was reported as "unsold and destroyed"
to the publisher, and neither the author nor the publisher
has received any payment for this "stripped" book.

The rest of the mice nodded. The terrible Tremaines—Lady Tremaine, Anastasia, and Drizella—had forced Cinderella to wait on them hand and foot after her father died. She'd been a servant in her very own home.

Then the King had thrown a ball so that he could introduce his son, the Prince, to all the young maidens in the kingdom. The mice had made Cinderella a beautiful outfit from an old dress that had belonged to her mother. But her stepsisters had destroyed it!

Luckily Cinderella's very own Fairy Godmother appeared. With a wave of her magic wand she transformed Bruno the dog (who now lay snoozing on a priceless carpet) into a footman and several of the mice into horses. She turned a pumpkin into a gleaming coach and Cinderella's tattered dress into a stunning blue ball gown.

Cinderella went to the ball. She and the Prince had danced and fallen in love. At midnight, she had to leave the ball quickly before everything turned back to normal. Luckily, she'd left behind a glass slipper. The Prince was able to find her. He hadn't cared that she was a servant, and the two had married.

A couple of months passed. Cinderella still couldn't believe how happy she was.

The castle clock—the very same one that had struck midnight on the night of the ball—began to chime. "Breakfast time!" Cinderella sang out merrily. "You know how the King hates it when anyone is late, especially at mealtimes!" She swung her legs out of bed and headed to the large window. She threw open the curtains, humming to herself. The birds in a nearby tree twittered their morning song. "Good morning!" Cinderella called to them.

She headed over to her wardrobe and looked inside. She reached in and picked out two dresses. One was purple with a lace hem and the other was pink silk with a full skirt.

"Wear the pink dress, Cinderelly!" Suzy exclaimed.

Cinderella blushed and put the purple dress back into the closet. "Certainly, Suzy!" she said. It was a good choice. She loved the way the skirt rustled when she walked. Two

of her bird friends flew in and tied the sash into a pretty bow. The princess brushed her blond hair until it shone. She slipped her feet into matching pink slippers.

"*Beeeautiful!*" said Perla.

"Thank you!" Cinderella replied, smiling. There was a knock at the door. Breakfast had arrived for the mice. As the princess's loyal friends, the mice were treated like royal guests. The maid began to set out tiny plates of tasty cheeses and grains, and Cinderella headed to breakfast.

"Good morning, Princess Cinderella," said the footman as she approached the dining room. He held open the carved door. "Thank you," she said. As she stepped inside, the Prince and the King stood. Their faces lit up when they saw her. Cinderella's heart leaped a bit when she saw her husband. She hid a smile when she noticed that the King had already tucked his napkin into his collar. He was eager to start the morning meal.

"There you are, daughter-in-law!" the King exclaimed. "Now we can eat."

The table was so large that it took the Prince a few moments to make his way to Cinderella's side. He clasped her hands in his. "Good morning, my love," he said, kissing her cheek.

"Good morning," Cinderella replied as the Prince pulled out her chair. She sat down, smoothing her skirt. The Prince, as you might imagine, had absolutely perfect manners.

"How did you sleep, my dear?" the King called.

"Very well, Your Highness," Cinderella replied.

"Come again?" the King responded. "Speak up. You're as quiet as a mouse!"

Cinderella giggled, thinking of her often-noisy mouse friends. She cupped her hands around her mouth. "I slept very well, Your Highness!" She practically had to shout to be heard. She didn't think she'd ever get used to this large room!

The King rang a bell, and the servants came in with the breakfast. And what a feast it was! Platter upon platter of eggs, pancakes, fruits, breads, and preserves. It was more food than the three of them could eat in a week, let alone in one meal. Another servant filled jeweled goblets with freshly squeezed juice.

The King grinned as he piled his plate with food. "It's good to be king!" he said and pounded the table with his fist for emphasis. His juice goblet flew into the air. It landed on its side, splashing orange liquid all over the tablecloth.

The King looked sheepish. "Oh dear. Look what I've done!"

Without thinking, Cinderella jumped to her feet, hurried over, and began mopping up the spill with her napkin. The King stared at her in surprise. One of the maids put down a platter and rushed over. "That's my job," she whispered kindly.

"Of course." Cinderella blushed as she walked to her side of the table. After she sat back down, she stole a glance at the Prince. He winked at her, which made her feel a tiny bit better. He understood that old habits were hard to break!

The King raised a finger solemnly. "Well, it certainly is a sorry day for the kingdom," he said.

"Why, Your Majesty?" Cinderella asked.

The King gave a jolly laugh. "Oh, it is just that you royal lovebirds will be parted today," he replied.

Cinderella and the Prince gave each other a sad smile. It was true. Today the Prince and the King would be leaving for an overnight visit to a neighboring kingdom.

It would be the first time Cinderella and the Prince would be apart since their wedding.

Just then the Grand Duke scurried into the room. He held a gold platter with a thick cream-colored envelope resting on it.

"Yes, yes, what do you want?" the King sputtered.

"A message, Your Majesty," he said, placing the envelope on the table.

The King frowned as he studied it. He reached out his hand, and the Grand Duke placed a solid gold letter opener in it. The King squinted at the raised red wax seal. "Could it be?" he said. He sliced the envelope open, fishing out a thick piece of white paper. "I . . . oh dear . . ."

As Cinderella watched, the King seemed
to get more and more upset.

"What is it, Father?" asked the Prince.

"This . . . this . . . this is terrible!" the King
moaned.

Chapter Two

"What's wrong?" asked the Prince. He rushed to his father's side. "Is it terrible news?"

The King frowned and pointed to the letter. The Grand Duke hovered behind him nervously.

The Prince picked up the letter. He glanced at his father. Then he decided to read it aloud.

My dear family,

It has been far too long since I last saw you. And I can hardly wait to meet the newest addition to the family— Cinderella! I arrive Wednesday in the late afternoon. Please have my usual rooms ready.

Love always,

Grandmama

Cinderella was confused. "Why, that's good news!" she said.

"It is," said the King. "She arrives this very evening. But I am upset because we won't be here to greet her. It has been months since I have seen my dear mama!"

The Prince shook his head. "It is sad to

miss even a day of her visit. But it cannot be avoided. We are expected in the neighboring kingdom today."

"Mama always does everything at the last minute," said the King, shaking his head. But he did so with a grin. "Well, I must be off. See you at the coach in ten minutes. Don't be late!" he said to his son. He stood, and the Grand Duke followed him out of the room.

"There's one good thing to come out of it," said the Prince, placing a hand on Cinderella's cheek. "You and Grandmama will be able to spend some time getting to know each other. By the time Father and I get back, you are sure to be the dearest of friends!"

Cinderella nodded. She *was* looking

forward to meeting the King's mother. She and the Prince had been disappointed that his beloved grandmother had not been able to attend their wedding. She had been visiting a kingdom far away and had not been able to get back in time.

The Prince took a second look at the letter. "There's more," he said. He cleared his throat. "'P.S. Please tell Cinderella I simply cannot wait to see her in the tiara I sent!'"

"Of course!" said Cinderella. "I will put it on right away." As a wedding gift, the Prince's grandmother had sent a sapphire tiara.

"You must wear it when you greet her," said the Prince.

"I will," promised Cinderella. "I want

everything to go perfectly this afternoon when I meet your grandmama."

"*Our* grandmama," said the Prince. "For she is sure to love you as much as I do."

"And I, her," said Cinderella.

The Prince frowned. "And now it is time for me to go," he said. "Will you see me to my coach?"

"Of course, my love," said Cinderella. They slowly walked to the front entrance of the castle together.

"I will see you soon, dearest," he said and kissed her.

"Into the coach, my son!" the King called from inside. "We must make haste!"

The Prince gave Cinderella one last glance and climbed inside.

"My goodness!" the King cried. "We're only going away for twenty-four hours, not twenty-four years!"

The horses took off. Cinderella stood and waved until the coach was out of sight.

She shielded her eyes and looked up at the palace clock. It was nearly time for her appointment with the royal dressmaker. They were going to look at some new dresses. After wearing the same rags for so long, Cinderella could hardly believe her good fortune. She was eager to see how they had turned out.

When Cinderella pushed open the drawing-room door, she found Chloe unpacking the dresses, which were in beautiful boxes. Chloe shared Cinderella's elegant taste in clothes and was wearing a simple silk gown in a rich dark-brown color. Cinderella smiled when she noticed that the lining, which you could only catch a peek of when Chloe walked, was a bright pink.

"Chloe, you look lovely!" said Cinderella.

"I simply can't wait to see the dresses you've created!"

"Oh, I had a wonderful time making them, I assure you!" said Chloe. She unwrapped the first dress and held it up for Cinderella to admire. Cinderella gasped when she saw the shimmery green gown. It had graceful bell-shaped sleeves.

"Oh!" said Cinderella, her eyes shining. She went behind a screen and slipped the dress over her head. Then she stepped in front of the mirror, her eyes lowered. The dressmaker's assistant fastened the ninety-nine satin-covered buttons that went up the back of the dress. Only then did Cinderella allow herself a peek at her reflection.

"It's . . . it's . . . it's . . . beautiful!" Cinderella said.

The dressmaker breathed a sigh of relief. "Thank you, Your Royal Highness!" she said. "But if I may say, you'd look beautiful even in rags!"

Cinderella smiled at that. Chloe had no idea!

Each dress was lovelier than the next. One was the color of a rosy sunrise and had a white lace overlay. A purple dress, its full skirt sprinkled with sequins, was fit for a ball. And a rich gold gown was embroidered with ivory thread.

The mice, who had stopped by for the

fashion show, were enthralled. "So beautiful, Cinderelly!" they cried.

"Thank you so much for creating such wonderful dresses!" Cinderella said warmly after she had tried on the last one. "You are so talented."

Chloe blushed with pleasure. She packed up the dresses to take back to her workshop—there was a hem to take up here and a waist to nip in there. She promised that the finished dresses would be delivered the following week.

Cinderella had a quick lunch of freshly baked French bread, cheese, and fruit (which she shared with the mice, of course). Then she decided to head to one of her favorite places in the palace—the princess garden.

She gathered her basket, her shears, and a large straw sun hat. She tied the long lilac ribbons under her chin.

Cinderella stepped outside into the bright sunlight and gazed around proudly. On her first day at the castle she had discovered a small garden. It had been quite wild and overgrown. The weeds outnumbered the flowers, and the fountain was hidden beneath a tangle of vines. Cinderella thought it would be fun to work on herself. She had started right away, trimming, replanting, and watering. In a short time, the garden had flourished.

Her bird friends built nests in the flowering trees and sang pretty songs for her as she pulled weeds and watered the thirsty plants. The mice sat in the shade of a bunch of bluebells. They so enjoyed watching Cinderella doing something that made her so happy.

Cinderella had an idea. "I know! I'll make a lovely bouquet to welcome Grandmama. What kind of flowers do you think she'll enjoy?" she asked the mice.

"Tulips?" suggested Jaq.

"Sunflowers?" said Gus, who loved the tasty seeds.

"Peonies?" added Perla.

"I know," said Cinderella. "Roses. You can't go wrong with roses. Everybody loves them." She pulled her clippers from her apron pocket and snipped dozens of roses. Soon, her basket was overflowing. Then she removed each and every thorn. After selecting a crystal vase from the greenhouse, she carefully arranged the sweet-smelling blooms.

"Perfect!" she said, holding the vase aloft. "Look at those colors. Pink like the rosy evening sky, yellow like freshly churned butter, peach like the sweetest fruit. And red like . . ."

"Sparkling rubies?" suggested Suzy.

"Rubies!" echoed Cinderella. "Nicely done, Suzy!" She thought for a moment. "That reminds me! It's time to find the tiara that Grandmama sent me. I really need to make a good first impression!"

Chapter Three

Taking one last sniff of the gorgeous blooms, Cinderella handed them to a footman. She asked him to place them in Grandmama's sitting room. Then she and the mice headed to her bedroom to find the tiara.

Cinderella looked around her room with pleasure. Warm afternoon sunlight streamed through the windows. Everything was arranged exactly the way she liked. "Now where did I put that tiara?" she wondered. She opened her jewelry box, which played a cheerful tune. Inside were several rings, a few bracelets, and a couple of necklaces. She snapped the box shut and then looked in her dresser, her desk drawers, and her nightstand. She even looked under the bed. No tiara. "Oh dear," she said. "Could it be missing?"

She walked over to the braided silk cord attached to a bell by her bed and pulled it. Within moments her lady's maid, a young woman named Marie Elise, appeared.

"Good afternoon, Princess," she said. "How may I help you?"

"I'm looking for one of my tiaras," replied Cinderella.

"Well, if it isn't in your jewelry box," the young maid told her, "then it can only be in the Royal Jewel Vault."

"The Royal Jewel what?" the princess asked wonderingly. There was so much about the castle that she still didn't know!

"Any jewelry that does not fit into your jewelry box is returned to the Royal Jewel Vault for safekeeping," explained Marie Elise. "That is where your tiara must be."

"Then I must go there immediately," Cinderella said. "Um . . . where is it?"

"I will take you there," said Marie Elise. She wrinkled her brow. "I'm surprised you haven't visited it yet. It is an amazing place. All of the royal jewels are stored there. Some of the pieces are hundreds and hundreds of years old."

"My goodness," said Cinderella. She turned to the mice. "Does anyone want to come with me?" she asked. Everyone did, of course. Except for Gus, who had fallen asleep on the window seat. Cinderella tucked a tiny blanket over the softly snoring mouse. "Sleep tight," she whispered.

Marie Elise led them into a wing of the castle they had never been to before. They passed room after room, their eyes taking in marble statues, stained glass windows, fancy carved furniture, chandeliers dripping with glittering crystals, thick carpets, and shiny suits of armor. Portraits of the Prince's ancestors lined the walls. They seemed to be watching Cinderella as she walked by.

Finally, at the end of a long hall, they arrived at a door with a huge lock on it. A large guard stood stiffly nearby.

"Enjoy the jewels!" Marie Elise called as she headed back down the hall.

"Thank you!" replied Cinderella. She could hardly wait to go inside.

Without a word, the guard removed an enormous golden key from a ring at his waist. He inserted and turned it. The heavy door swung open with a loud creak.

As the guard began to light the room, Cinderella tiptoed inside. The walls were covered in fancy wallpaper. There was a thick magenta carpet on the floor, which muffled her footsteps. The room was lined with glass cases. She stepped forward and peered inside one of them, gasping in disbelief as her eyes lit upon a huge crown with rubies as big as plums. Who would be able to hold their head up under a heavy crown like that!

The magnificent jewels on display made Cinderella feel as if she were in a museum. She found herself tiptoeing, her hands behind her back, afraid to touch anything.

She paused in front of a case full of rings. There had to be hundreds of them. Another case was filled with bracelets; the next two were devoted to necklaces. Another held jeweled combs and hairpins.

On top of one glass case sat a velvet tray of rings with different colored stones. Deep

red rubies, fresh green emeralds, milky white pearls, black pearls, diamonds in every color of the rainbow.

Jaq climbed up to take a look. "Don't be afraid," he said as Cinderella started to reach out to touch a heavy gold ring with a robin's-egg-blue topaz. It was about the size and shape of an actual robin's egg, too. "You're the princess. It's all yours!"

"He's right, you know," said a voice. "I was wondering when you would pay us a visit."

Cinderella turned with a start. There stood an official-looking older man. Both his voice and eyes were kind. "Welcome to the Royal Jewel Vault, my dear."

"Why thank you!" said Cinderella.

"I am Pierre, the royal jeweler," he said. "How may I help you today? Do you need a purple diamond cocktail ring to wear to a fancy dinner party? A sapphire necklace to match your lovely eyes? A moonstone brooch for a midnight picnic under the stars?"

"My goodness, that sounds wonderful!" said Cinderella. "But I am actually looking for a tiara."

"We keep those in the Tiara Room," explained the jeweler. "Are you interested in gold, platinum, or silver?" he asked. "Or pearls, opals, diamonds, emeralds, rubies, sapphires, or garnets?"

Cinderella felt as if her head was spinning. "Actually, I am looking for a special tiara," she said. "I received it from the Prince's grandmother. It is platinum with a large sapphire heart."

The jeweler nodded. "I'll be right back," he said. While he was gone, Cinderella got up the nerve to try on some jewelry. She slipped on an amethyst bracelet. She admired herself in the mirror, before swapping it for an emerald and diamond necklace. The mice held a pair of sparkling grape-colored

garnet earrings to her ears and stared at her reflection.

Finally Pierre returned, a red leather box in his hands. He placed it on the counter in front of Cinderella.

Cinderella took a deep breath. Then she unfastened the clasp and lifted the lid.

"I can't believe it!" she cried.

Chapter Four

"What is it, Cinderelly?" Jaq squeaked. The rest of the mice, who had been busily exploring the glass cases, scampered to her side.

Cinderella was so upset she didn't even notice that little Mert was off balance under the weight of a large ring, which he had placed on his head like a crown.

"Is something wrong?" Pierre asked,

concerned. Cinderella held up the velvet-lined box. It was empty.

The mice gasped. So did Pierre.

"Could the tiara have been put into another jewel box by mistake?" Cinderella asked when she was finally able to speak.

The jeweler shook his head. "Impossible," he said. "We have a foolproof system in the Royal Jewel Vault. It has been in place for hundreds of years. If the tiara is not in its box, then it was never returned."

Cinderella shook her head sadly. "Well then, where could it be?" she wondered aloud. She had a sudden, horrifying thought. "You don't think it could have been . . . stolen, do you?" she asked Pierre.

The Royal Jeweler laughed. "This

castle has guards all over the place," he said. "That is highly unlikely. It must have been misplaced."

Jaq rolled up his sleeves. "Well, then it's got to be somewhere in the castle," he said. "Let the royal search begin!"

Cinderella nodded. "Thank you, Pierre," she said as she and the mice turned to leave.

"Good luck, Princess," said Pierre.

"Thank you," said Cinderella. "I have a feeling I'll need it."

They made their way back to the princess's room. "We will begin our search," Cinderella told the mice. "But I have to ask you to keep this our little secret. I can't take the chance that Grandmama will find out I have misplaced her gift."

Gus spoke up. "Always best to tell the truth."

Cinderella bit her lip. "I don't mean that we should lie," she said slowly. "Just that maybe we can hold off telling Grandmama about this until it is necessary."

The mice nodded, though Gus still did not look convinced.

The castle was quite large, and they searched for a very long time. They looked under tables, behind curtains, and beneath carpets. And in every drawer, shelf, and closet. But no tiara.

Cinderella was on her hands and knees in the parlor when the door creaked open. The housekeeper stepped inside to do some last-minute dusting before Grandmama's

arrival. "Oh my goodness!" she gasped when she spotted the princess on her hands and knees poking underneath a table.

Cinderella looked up. She thought quickly. "Hello!" she cried merrily. "I'm just playing a game with the mice!"

She was startled when the usually serious housekeeper shrugged her shoulders. "Sounds like fun!" she said. The next thing Cinderella knew, the woman got down on all fours and began peering under the furniture, too! "Is this how you play?" she asked.

Not knowing what else to do, Cinderella smiled and continued her search.

It was clear that the tiara was not in the parlor. But Cinderella was not quite sure how to end the "game." Finally she had an idea. "Oh, I give up. You win!" she said, standing up.

The housekeeper looked very confused. "Well, that wasn't a very fun game at all," she muttered as Cinderella and the mice left the room.

They continued their search. They looked among the plants in the garden. Inside the

grand piano. In every pot and pan and bowl in the kitchen.

"I give up!" Cinderella finally said, meaning it this time, as she replaced the final book in the library. She had a smudge of dust on one cheek, and her dress was wrinkled.

"Okay, Cinderelly," said the mice. They had had enough, too.

She glanced at the grandfather clock. It was getting late. "Oh, dear, we don't have much time to prepare for Grandmama's arrival," she said, her hands flying to her messy hair. "Let's hurry!"

The group quickly made their way back to Cinderella's room. As they rounded a corner, they ran smack into Gus. He had a panicked look on his face.

"What's wrong, Gus-Gus?" asked Perla. "Tell us!"

"Cinderelly! Cinderelly!" he burst out. "Come quick!"

"What is it?" she asked the little mouse.

"There's an intruder in your room—going through your jewelry box!"

Chapter Five

Cinderella gasped. "Help! Help!" she cried. She ran down the hallway as fast as her pink satin slippers would carry her. Without a second thought, she threw open the door to her room.

"Is anyone there?" she cried out.

Three large guards raced to help her. "Let us take care of this." Cinderella stepped aside.

"Halt! Who goes there!" one of them shouted.

Then there was a bit of a commotion, some talking, and was that . . . laughing she heard? Cinderella tried to see in, but the guards were blocking her view. What was happening?

The guards came into the hallway. They were laughing and joking. A sweet-looking older woman clutching a large bag walked behind them.

"Can you imagine?" one of them said. "We thought it was an intruder, but it was really Grandmama!"

Cinderella's mouth fell open. Had she really sent the palace guards after the Prince's grandmother?

"A thousand pardons, Your Royal Highness," said one of the guards.

"No, I am the one who should be doing the apologizing," said Grandmama, smiling at the crowd that had gathered. Everyone, it seemed, was delighted to see her. "Can you believe I got lost in my own family's home?" she asked. Everyone laughed merrily.

She turned to Cinderella and squinted at her. "You must be my new granddaughter," she said.

"I am," replied Cinderella. "It is a pleasure to make your acq—"

"Yes, yes. You too. So where is the tiara I sent you?" she asked eagerly. "I was hoping to see it . . . I mean, to see how wonderful it looks on you."

Cinderella gulped. "Soon," she said. "Very soon."

Grandmama frowned and clutched her large purse closer to her side. "Such a disappointment. I had better head to my room then," she said.

The crowd began to drift away. "Poor Grandmama!" Cinderella heard someone say. She felt very terrible indeed.

Cinderella hurried down the hallway after Grandmama. "I apologize that the Prince and the King are not here," she said. "They will be back from their trip tomorrow evening and cannot wait to see you."

Grandmama barely nodded. She appeared to be deep in thought.

"I hope you are hungry!" Cinderella said.

"Cook is preparing a wonderful meal with all of your favorite dishes."

"That sounds lovely," Grandmama said distractedly.

When they got to her room, Grandmama stepped inside and closed the door, leaving Cinderella behind in the hallway. "Well, I guess I'll see you at dinner!" she called out.

As she started to leave, she heard a door open. Cinderella turned around. There stood Grandmama, holding the vase full

of the flowers Cinderella had picked. The princess smiled.

Grandmama thrust the vase into the hands of a passing footman. "Imagine!" she said to him. "Somebody put *roses* in my room!"

The guard clucked his tongue.

She shook her head. "Everyone knows I am highly allergic!" She turned and closed the door behind her with a loud click.

Cinderella bit her lip.

"Well, that didn't go very well," said Gus.

"You can say that again," said Mert.

"Well, that didn't go very well," Gus repeated.

Everybody groaned.

Chapter Six

Cinderella was relieved when Grandmama said that she was too tired for a formal meal. So they both ate dinner in their own quarters.

"I am sorry not to be able to spend time with Grandmama," Cinderella told the mice. "But it is a relief not to have to answer questions about the tiara!"

Gus and Suzy nodded.

"If only I could remember the last place I wore it!" said Cinderella. "Surely the Prince will be able to help me. Then I can make everything right with Grandmama."

"He won't be back tonight," Jaq reminded her.

"You're right. I suppose I can't avoid her all day tomorrow," said Cinderella. "Though it is tempting!"

The mice all held their paws to their mouths and giggled.

"No, I need to figure out something enjoyable for us to do together tomorrow to pass the time until the Prince and the King return," Cinderella said.

"A carriage ride?" suggested Mert.

Cinderella shook her head. "Too much

opportunity to talk about tiaras!" she said.

Jaq had an idea. "Oh, there's a new play at the theater!"

Cinderella brightened. "Yes, one of the maids did mention that. What a wonderful idea!"

Jaq looked very pleased with himself. When he asked if he and Gus could go along in her purse, Cinderella readily agreed.

Cinderella put on a nightdress with pink embroidery and a matching bed jacket. And as she put her head on the pillow, she thought to herself, I will have a pleasant day with Grandmama tomorrow. And hopefully I'll remember when I last wore her tiara. But then her face burned with embarrassment as she remembered that she had called the guards on the Prince's grandmother. And then she had a sudden thought before she drifted off to sleep: Grandmama grew up in this castle. How exactly did she get lost? Just what *was* she doing in my room?

"I haven't been to the theater in ages!" said Grandmama as she settled into her seat. She looked about the Royal Box approvingly. There were heavy velvet curtains, plush red seats, and several pairs of opera glasses at the ready. They were the very best seats in the house.

Cinderella smiled. The carriage ride to the theater had been uneventful. At one moment it seemed as if Grandmama was

about to ask why she wasn't wearing the
tiara. But Cinderella quickly changed the
subject. Somehow, she kept the conversation
going until they arrived at the theater.
Halfway there, Cinderella opened her bag
to introduce Jaq and Gus to Grandmama,
but discovered that the little mice were
napping. She closed her bag with a snap.
She'd save that for later.

In the Royal Box, Grandmama squinted at her program. "Oh, they are performing *The Royal Riddle!*" she said excitedly. "I've heard wonderful things about it. I can hardly wait to see it." She frowned and began to root around in her bag. "I know my glasses are in here somewhere. . . ."

Cinderella reached for the bag. "Let me help you," she offered.

Grandmama snatched the bag away. "I can do it myself! Please don't touch my bag," she said.

"I'm sorry," said Cinderella. She seemed to do everything wrong when it came to Grandmama! They were still standing, and the play was starting. "Well," she whispered after a moment, "I've heard the play is quite

good myself." She patted the empty velvet seat to her right. "I'm also happy that the Royal Box has been repaired. The last time we came here there had been a rainstorm the night before. There was a leak in the roof, and the Royal Box was flooded. So we had to sit in different seats."

Grandmama nodded absently as she searched through her large bag again.

Cinderella looked at the princess onstage and gasped. The missing tiara was on her head!

Chapter Seven

Cinderella glanced over at Grandmama. Luckily, she still hadn't found her glasses and couldn't recognize the tiara. But then she reached for the opera glasses. Cinderella had to think fast!

The princess tapped Grandmama on the shoulder.

Grandmama looked up at her, surprised. "Pardon me?" she said.

"I changed my mind!" Cinderella whispered in a rush. "We can see a play anytime! Let's go to the tea salon instead!"

"But . . . but . . ."

The princess helped Grandmama to her feet. "I'm sorry, I'm just very, very thirsty for some tea!" she said. Shaking her head, Grandmama allowed herself to be led out of the theater and into the waiting carriage.

"This is highly unusual," Grandmama muttered as she climbed inside. "Highly!"

Cinderella stepped in and closed the door behind her. "To the tea salon!" she told the footman. She would have to return to the theater later to retrieve the tiara. But at least she had found it!

As the carriage set off, Cinderella noticed

Grandmama's puzzled expression. She felt bad that she was being so dishonest with Grandmama. But it would all be over soon.

"This is lovely!" said Grandmama once they were seated in the tea salon. She narrowed her eyes at Cinderella. "I trust we will be staying here for more than five minutes?"

"I . . . um . . ." Cinderella began.

Luckily, Grandmama was distracted by the pastries that had arrived at their table. The waiter placed a tray of pastries filled with custard and delicate cakes and cookies.

From inside Cinderella's purse, Gus sniffed the air. He rubbed his round belly.

"Wait," said Jaq. "Cinderelly will get us when she's ready."

But Gus was tired of waiting. And he was very, very hungry. He poked his head out of the purse. *Aha!* He spotted a cookie with chocolate icing. He sneaked across the table to claim it.

Cinderella did not see her little friend. "Cupcake?" she asked Grandmama.

"Don't mind if I do," said Grandmama, whose good spirits had returned at the sight of the pastries. Cinderella extended the plate to Grandmama—and there, to her surprise, sat Gus!

Grandmama's mouth fell open in shock. She put her hands on the table and stood up, knocking over the teapot. Tea spilled

everywhere. The tablecloth was soaked. Grandmama pointed to the plate. "It's . . . a . . . a . . . a . . . mouse!" she shouted.

Ladies screamed and one gentleman jumped up on his chair in fright. A waitress came rushing over. "Oh my goodness!" he cried. "Begging your pardon, Your Highness!" Then he looked down at little Gus, sitting happily on the plate.

"Oh, it's just Gus!" he said in relief. "Everybody, no need to worry. It is only Princess Cinderella's little friend."

Grandmama took a closer look. "Is that mouse wearing . . . clothes?" she asked incredulously.

"Another cookie, please!" said Gus.

"You could have told me you had mouse

friends!" Grandmama said, shaking her head. She raised her cup of tea to Jaq and Gus. "Pleased to meet you both," she said.

"Pleased to meet you, Your Highness," they squeaked.

The table had been cleared and a fresh pot of tea brewed. Grandmama had sent pastries to every table in the shop to make up for the disturbance.

Everything was back to normal. But Cinderella had lost her appetite.

She had called the guards on Grandmama, offered her roses, left the play early, and nearly scared her half to death. Not to mention losing the tiara. Cinderella was sure the Prince's grandmother couldn't possibly like her.

After they left the tea shop and were settled into the carriage, Cinderella leaned forward. "To the theater, please," she told the driver.

Grandmama raised an eyebrow.

"I need to get something I left behind," the princess explained. She sighed. This would all be over soon. Then maybe she and Grandmama could start again from scratch.

***

"Princess Cinderella!" whispered one of the ushers when Cinderella walked into the theater. "You left in such a hurry. However can I help you?"

"I need to speak with the actress who

played the princess!" said Cinderella in a low voice. "It's very important!"

The usher nodded. "Her part is finished. She's backstage. Please follow me."

"Yes, of course," said Cinderella.

They went to the lobby, and the usher opened the door to the stage. Cinderella looked around wonderingly. She had never been backstage before. The ropes, pulleys, and piles of scenery were very interesting to see indeed.

The actress was thrilled to meet her. "Princess Cinderella!" she cried in surprise, dropping to a deep curtsy. "What an honor!"

"It's always an honor for me to meet another princess," Cinderella replied with a smile.

Cinderella took a closer look at the tiara the actress was wearing. Her mouth dropped open. It wasn't the missing tiara at all! Had she been mistaken?

"Is something wrong?" asked the actress.

"I just . . . I just thought that you were wearing a different tiara onstage," she said.

"You have an eye for detail!" said the actress. "Indeed, I was. But when I was racing backstage between scenes I dropped the crown and someone rolled a cart over it. We had to substitute a different one." She smiled. "I was hoping no one would notice!"

Cinderella's heart sank. The tiara was damaged! "Where is the crown now?" she asked.

"I'm not sure if the prop mistress can

repair it," the actress said. "She's in the prop room if you want to check."

Cinderella knocked on the prop-room door. Hearing nothing, she pushed the door open. Inside, a woman with dark hair and round glasses was polishing a fake sword. She stepped forward as the door opened. "Who goes there?" she said jokingly.

The prop mistress's face lit up when she saw it was Cinderella. She curtsied. "Princess Cinderella!" she said. "What can I do for you?"

"I am here about the tiara that the actress playing the princess was wearing," explained Cinderella. "I have reason to think that it belongs to me. She told me it was damaged and returned to you."

"Oh dear," said the prop mistress. "The tiara was so damaged, I threw it out. Begging your pardon, but I had no idea it was real!" She shook her head in disbelief. "I can't believe I threw out your tiara! We must find it immediately." She headed out of the prop room.

Cinderella followed her down the hallway.

The prop mistress turned around and looked at Cinderella over her round glasses. "If I may ask, how did your crown end up in my prop room?"

Cinderella gave a quick laugh. "It is odd, isn't it?" she said. "I think I have it figured out. When we came last week, the Royal Box was closed for repairs. So the Prince and I were seated in the orchestra. When I turned around, I noticed that I was sitting in front of a young girl. I realized my tiara was blocking her view. So I removed it and placed it carefully under my seat. But then I forgot to put it back on before I left."

"I wonder if someone accidentally kicked it," said the prop mistress.

"That's exactly what I was thinking!"

said Cinderella. "And then it rolled down by the stage. An usher must have picked it up, thought it was a prop, and put it in the prop room."

The prop mistress shook her head. "I knew I didn't recognize it! Come with me." She pushed open a door, which led into an alley. "I put it right out here." She pointed to a garbage bin just outside the door.

Cinderella smiled. But her grin quickly faded. The tiara was nowhere to be seen.

Chapter Eight

"Oh dear," the prop mistress said sadly. "Someone must have taken it. I am so sorry, Your Highness. And now I must get back to prepare for the next scene!"

Cinderella bid the prop mistress farewell. She slowly headed back to the carriage. How was she going to tell the Prince's beloved grandmother that the priceless tiara she had given her was last seen in a garbage barrel?

Sadly, she climbed inside the carriage and sat across from Grandmama.

"Home, please," she called to the driver. She took a deep breath. "Grandmama," she said. "I have a confession to make."

"Don't do it!" squeaked Jaq.

Gus covered Jaq's mouth with his paw.

"I . . . I . . . I lost the tiara you sent me," said Cinderella. "And I've been trying to

keep it from you since you arrived." She told Grandmama the whole story. Then she hung her head with shame.

Grandmama looked very, very surprised. In fact, she was speechless.

"I am so sorry, Grandmama!" Cinderella cried. "How will you ever forgive me?"

Grandmama spoke up. "Actually, there is nothing—"

"I know!" cried Cinderella. "There is nothing I can do to make this up to you."

"No, what I mean is—" Grandmama began. She took a deep breath.

Just then, out of the corner of her eye, Cinderella spotted a group of girls standing together on the street. One of them appeared to be crying and was wearing a blanket around her shoulders. She took a closer look. The blanket looked like a makeshift cape. Another wore a daisy-chain crown on her head. They were obviously playing princess. Could *they* have taken her crown?

"Stop the carriage!" Cinderella cried.

She jumped out of the carriage and ran over to the girls.

"Excuse me!" she called.

"It's the princess!" one of the girls shouted. The others squealed with delight. They had never been so close to a real princess before.

"Why are you crying?" Cinderella gently asked the red-eyed girl.

"A mean boy just stole my crown!" she said with a sniff.

Cinderella's heart skipped a beat. "Was it a gold crown with a blue heart?" she asked.

The little girl's eyes widened. "It was!"

"I think it might be my tiara," said Cinderella.

"Oh no!" The girl shook her head adamantly. "We found it in the garbage. It couldn't possibly be yours."

Cinderella gave a small laugh. "Oh, you'd be surprised! Where did the boy take it?"

"Well, he said he was going to put it somewhere we couldn't get it!" the girl with the daisy-chain crown explained.

"Which way did he go?" asked Cinderella.

"This way!" Two of the girls grabbed Cinderella's hands and pulled her down the street toward a small park. A statue of the

King stood in the center. Cinderella shielded her eyes against the sun and looked up at her father-in-law.

Cinderella blinked in amazement at what she saw. "Oh my goodness!" she cried. "It's the tiara!"

The girls looked up. "That boy was right," said the crying girl. "We'll never get it!"

Just then Grandmama joined them, with Jaq and Gus.

Cinderella pointed up at the tiara. "There it is," she said to Grandmama. "I'm so sorry."

Grandmama was surprisingly cheerful. "We'll send someone from the castle to get it later. Let's go." She seemed to be in a big rush.

Cinderella shook her head. "No, we need to get it now. This is all my fault."

A butcher came out of his shop, wiping his hands on his apron. "Your Majesties," he said. "I would be happy to get the tiara for you. I will borrow a ladder from the roofer as soon as he returns. Shouldn't be more than a few hours." He smiled and walked back into his shop.

"Very sensible," said Grandmama. "Now let's get back to the castle. . . ."

"No," said Cinderella. "We've come this far. We're so close. I must get it now." And then to the disbelieving eyes of Grandmama, Jaq, Gus, and the girls, she dragged over an apple crate from in front of the butcher's store, picked up a long stick, gathered her skirts, and began to climb to the base of the statue!

"Be careful, Princess!" called the girls.

"Cinderella! Please get down!" shouted Grandmama. "What in the world are you doing? This is too dangerous!"

Cinderella was now standing on the base of the statue. She steadied herself by leaning on the King's leg and began to reach up with the stick. "Oh dear," she said as she wobbled a bit.

"STOP!" yelled Grandmama. "I can't let this go on another moment!"

Chapter Nine

Cinderella turned around, her mouth a round "o" of surprise. "What is wrong, Grandmama?" she asked.

Grandmama gazed at the ground, looking embarrassed. "Now it is I who has a confession to make," she said softly.

Cinderella climbed down from the statue and put her hand on Grandmama's arm. "It's all right," she said. "Tell me what's wrong."

Grandmama reached into her large purse and removed a velvet bag. She loosened the drawstrings and pulled out—the very same crown that was on the King's statue.

Everyone gasped.

"Now I'm really confused," said Gus.

"Tell me about it," replied Jaq.

"I . . . I . . . don't understand," said Cinderella looking from one tiara to the other.

"I always do everything at the last minute," Grandmama said miserably. "I thought this time it would be different. I planned to give you a one-of-a-kind tiara with a sapphire heart for your wedding present. But I went to the jeweler too late! There wasn't enough time to find the perfect sapphire. So rather than sending the present late, I asked the jeweler to make a fake tiara, which I sent to you. I figured I could switch it with the real one when I came for my visit, and no one would know."

"So *that's* why you were in my room when you first arrived," said Cinderella. "You weren't lost at all!"

Grandmama laughed. "No, I wasn't! As soon as I got to the castle I tried to find the tiara and make the switch," she said. "And you caught me."

"And it wasn't even there!" added Cinderella. Her shoulders began to shake. She wiped her eyes with her white lace handkerchief.

"Don't cry, Princess!" said one of the girls.

"Oh, I am so sorry!" cried Grandmama. "I should have just told you right away. Things wouldn't have gotten so out of hand."

"I'm not upset," said Cinderella, trying to catch her breath. "It's really very funny, isn't it? That's why I'm laughing so hard!"

"Oh!" said Grandmama, relieved. And then she began to laugh, too. "What two foolish people we were. Trying to keep secrets from one another!"

"Always best to tell the truth," said Gus solemnly.

"That's what my mother always says," offered the girl with the daisy-chain crown.

Cinderella wiped her eyes and nodded. "You were right, Gus," she told him. "I really should have listened."

Gus looked very surprised. It wasn't all that often that he was right. He elbowed Jaq in the ribs to make sure he'd heard.

Jaq smiled. "You *were* right, Gus-Gus!"

Cinderella got serious all of a sudden. "So," she said. "May I try on the tiara now?"

"Of course, my dear!" Grandmama placed the tiara on Cinderella's head.

The little girls gasped. "So beautiful!"

"It's almost as beautiful as you are," said

Grandmama. She put a hand on Cinderella's shoulder. "I am so sorry we got off on the wrong foot. All because of my silly pride."

"Mine too," admitted Cinderella. She hugged Grandmama tightly.

"There you are!" called a familiar voice. It was the Prince on horseback! "Father and I just returned." He dismounted and hugged them both hello. "I trust you two had a lovely visit."

"The Prince!" shouted the girls. This was a very special day for them indeed.

"It was quite an adventure!" Cinderella said. Puzzled, the Prince looked at her, but then his eye was caught by the glittering crown on the statue's head. He looked from it to Cinderella and back again.

"Is there any reason why my father's statue is wearing the same tiara as my wife?" he asked in confusion.

Everyone laughed and laughed. "It's a long story!" Grandmama told him when she had caught her breath. "We'll tell it to you sometime!"

He shook his head. "I'm just glad my two favorite people are getting along so well."

"We most certainly are!" said Cinderella. "It turns out that Grandmama and I have a lot more in common than we first thought!"

Cinderella smiled at Grandmama, who winked back at her. Now that the two were friends, Cinderella knew that this was only the beginning of the many adventures they would have together.

Don't miss the next Disney Princess Jewel Story!

Belle
The Charming Gift

Belle and the Beast have decided to hold a winter ball at the castle! While Belle decides what to wear, she is reminded of the special charm bracelet her father made for her. Mrs. Potts and the rest of the enchanted objects notice that Belle is sad and decide to make her a new bracelet. Everyone has to scramble to find the perfect jewels for their charms. Will Belle's surprise be finished in time—and what will the Beast have to say about it?